Welcome to ALADDIN QUIX!

If you are looking for fast, fun-to-read stories with colorful characters, lots of kid-friendly humor, easy-to-follow action, entertaining story lines, and lively illustrations, then **ALADDIN QUIX** is for you!

But wait, there's more!

If you're also looking for stories with tables of contents; word lists; about-the-book questions; 64, 80, or 96 pages; short chapters; short paragraphs; and large fonts, then **ALADDIN QUIX** is *definitely* for you!

ALADDIN QUIX: The next step between ready to reads and longer, more challenging chapter books, for readers five to eight years old.

The Best Friend Plan

Read more ALADDIN QUIX books!

By Stephanie Calmenson

Our Principal Is a Frog!
Our Principal Is a Wolf!
Our Principal's in His Underwear!
Our Principal Breaks a Spell!

The Adventures of
ALLIE and AMY
The Best Friend Plan

By Stephanie Calmenson and Joanna Cole
Illustrated by James Burks

ALADDIN QUIX

New York London Toronto Sydney New Delhi

ALADDIN QUIX
Simon & Schuster Children's Publishing Division
1230 Avenue of the Americas, New York, New York 10020
First Aladdin QUIX hardcover edition January 2020
Text copyright © 1995 by Joanna Cole and Stephanie Calmenson
Illustrations copyright © 2020 by James Burks
The text of this book was originally published in slightly
different form as *The Gator Girls* (1995).
Also available in an Aladdin QUIX paperback edition.
All rights reserved, including the right of reproduction in whole or in part in any form.
ALADDIN and the related marks and colophon are trademarks of Simon & Schuster, Inc.
For information about special discounts for bulk purchases, please contact
Simon & Schuster Special Sales at 1-866-506-1949 or business@simonandschuster.com.
The Simon & Schuster Speakers Bureau can bring authors to your live event. For
more information or to book an event contact the Simon & Schuster Speakers Bureau
at 1-866-248-3049 or visit our website at www.simonspeakers.com.
Designed by Heather Palisi
The illustrations for this book were rendered digitally.
The text of this book was set in Archer Medium.
Manufactured in the United States of America 1219 LAK
2 4 6 8 10 9 7 5 3 1
Library of Congress Control Number 2019938115
ISBN 978-1-5344-5251-0 (hc)
ISBN 978-1-5344-5250-3 (pbk)
ISBN 978-1-5344-5252-7 (eBook)

To each other

—S. C. and J. C.

Cast of Characters

Amy Cooper: Allie Anderson's best friend

Allie Anderson: Amy Cooper's best friend

Madame Lulu: Fortune-teller who is really Mrs. Suzie Tompkins, a neighbor in Allie's building

Marvin Lopez: A boy who's sometimes fun and sometimes annoying

Contents

1

Guess Who!

Ring! Ring! Early one morning, the telephone rang at **Amy Cooper**'s house. Amy's mother answered it.

"It's for you, Amy," she called. "Guess who!"

Amy had no trouble guessing.
She knew it was her best friend,
Allie Anderson.

"Meet me downstairs!" said Allie. "We've got to talk."

"Aren't we talking now?" said Amy.

"We've got to talk face-to-face, nose-to-nose, eyeball-to-eyeball!" said Allie.

"I'm on my way!" said Amy.

Amy raced to the elevator in her apartment building. She lived on the sixth floor. She watched the floor numbers light up: *six, five, four, three, two, one.* **"Hurry, hurry,"** she said.

As soon as the elevator doors opened, she **burst** outside and ran to Allie's building right next door.

Just like Amy, Allie lived on the sixth floor. Just like Amy, Allie watched the floor numbers light up: *six, five, four, three, two, one.*

"Ta-da!" she said, bursting out the door. "Are you ready for our first day of summer vacation? Remember, we've got big plans!"

"I remember and I'm ready," said Amy. "Did you bring the list?"

"It's right here," said Allie, pulling a **crumpled** paper out of her pocket. She began to read.

THINGS TO DO THIS SUMMER

1. Get our fortunes told by Madame Lulu
2. Go to the Spring Street Fair
3. Skate and sing backward
4. Swim at the town pool
5. Make a new list of things to do

"Wow. We're going to be busy," said Amy.

"We'd better get started right away," said Allie. "**Madame Lulu**, here we come!"

2

Madame Lulu

Allie and Amy went around the corner to Madame Lulu's Fortune-Telling Parlor. It was pink and yellow outside, but dark and a little spooky inside.

Even though the girls knew

that Madame Lulu was nice Mrs. Tompkins from the first floor of Allie's building, they still got the **shivers** going inside.

"You go in first," said Allie, taking a step back.

"No, you," said Amy, taking two steps back.

"No, you," said Allie, taking three steps back.

"Greetings, fortune **seekers**," called a **husky** voice from the dark. "Why don't you *both* come inside?"

Allie and Amy held hands and squeezed through the doorway together.

Madame Lulu sat behind a beaded curtain. She was dressed in black with a **veil** on her head.

She had about twenty brace-
lets on each arm. They clinked
together whenever she moved.

"What brings you here?" she
asked. **Clink!**

"W-w-we want our fortunes
told," said Amy.

Amy and Allie each held out a
coin to Madame Lulu.

Madame Lulu slipped the coins
into her pocket. **Clink!**

"Can you tell us what the summer
is going to be like?" asked Allie.

"Of course," said Madame Lulu.

She gazed into her crystal ball. "The summer will be **hazy**, hot, and **humid**," she said. "In fact, it already is."

Madame Lulu wiped the sweat off her forehead with a lace handkerchief. **_Clink!_**

Allie and Amy looked at each other.

"Thanks, but that's not what we meant," said Amy. "We don't need to know about the weather. We need to know about *us*."

She poked Allie, who put another coin on the table. Madame Lulu took the coin. ***Clink!***

"Let me see your **palms**," she said.

Allie and Amy turned their palms up and held them out.

"Hmm, nice and clean," said

Madame Lulu. "And do you moisturize?"

"Um, no, we don't," said Allie. "You're going to tell our fortunes, right?"

"**Absolutely!** One best friends fortune coming right up," said Madame Lulu. "I see an interesting story. Today is a special day. It's . . . It's coming to me now."

Madame Lulu closed her eyes and held her fingers to her brow.

Going into a **trance**, she said, "Today is . . . the very first day . . .

of your summer vacation!"

"**Wow!** How did she know that?" whispered Amy.

Madame Lulu continued. "You will take a trip to a special place. I see sun shining. I hear water splashing. I smell hot dogs cooking on an open fire."

Suddenly Madame Lulu snapped out of her trance. "Did someone say 'hot dogs'?" she asked.

"You did," said Allie and Amy together.

Madame Lulu looked at her

watch. "Ah, yes. It's time for my coffee break," she said.

Allie and Amy had no more coins anyway. They walked through the beaded curtain and out into the hazy, hot, and humid day.

Boom! They bumped right into a boy named . . .

"MARVIN!!!"

Amy yelled, "Why don't you watch where you're going?"

"Watch where *I'm* going?" said **Marvin Lopez.**

He checked his skateboard for scratches. "Watch where *you're* going. You're the ones who bumped into me!"

"Well, don't do it again," said Allie.

Allie, Amy, and Marvin could go round and round being silly all day long. But Allie and Amy had no time for that today.

They put their noses in the air, linked arms, and headed for home.

"See you later, alligator," said Amy, going into her building.

"In a while, crocodile," said Allie, going into hers.

3

Camp Merry Moose

Allie's father and mother were waiting for her when she walked in the door.

"Hi, honey," said her mother, with a big smile.

"We have wonderful news for you!" said her father.

"What is it?" asked Allie.

"Remember that camp you wanted to go to? The one we talked about last winter?" said her mother.

Allie **perked** up. "You mean Camp Merry Moose? Where they have sailboats and everything?" she said.

"That's the one," said Allie's father.

"I thought there was no room for me. I thought it was all filled up," said Allie.

"There was a last-minute opening. So now you can go!" said Allie's mother. "Camp starts the day after tomorrow."

Allie could hardly believe it.

She had always wanted to go to sleepaway camp. Sunshine, swimming, campfires. **Wow!** This had to be the special place Madame Lulu was talking about. Allie was so happy, she wanted to tell Amy right away!

Ring! Ring! The telephone rang at Amy's house. Amy's father answered it.

"It's for you, Amy," he said. **"Guess who!"**

Amy had no trouble guessing.

"Hi, Allie," she said. "I haven't

talked to you in five whole minutes. What's new?"

"What's new? Front-page news!" shouted Allie. "My parents just told me I'm going to Camp Merry Moose! I'm going for the whole summer! There's a lake with boats, and everyone gets to sleep in a tent."

Amy was so surprised, she didn't say anything for a minute. Then she burst out, "You can't go to camp. Not without me! We're best friends. **We have plans!**"

"Oh my gosh, you're right!" **yelped** Allie. "I was so excited, I forgot you weren't going. **I can't go to camp without you!**"

"That's right," said Amy. "You can't. But maybe I can go too. I'll ask my parents."

"That won't work. There was only one space, and my parents got it for me," said Allie sadly. "But wait. I know what to do. I'll call you back."

Allie hung up and found her parents.

"I can't go to camp," she said. "I'm staying home with Amy."

"Allie, you have to go," said her mother. "We made all the arrangements."

"But Amy and I do everything together," said Allie.

"You and Amy can write to each other," said her father.

"You'll have a wonderful time at camp," said her mother.

"No, I won't," said Allie. "Not without Amy I won't."

"Well, you have to give it a

chance," said her father. "You're going, and that's final."

Allie walked slowly to her room. She sat down on her bed to think. A minute later, she popped up, raced to the phone, and dialed Amy's number.

"Meet me downstairs. We've got to talk," she said.

"Okay," said Amy. "I'm on my way."

Six, five, four, three, two, one. Allie and Amy burst out of their doors at the exact same moment.

4

Allie's Plan

"I've got a plan," said Allie. "It's great. It's the best. **I'm a genius. You won't believe it....**"

"Well, I can't believe it if I don't hear it," said Amy. "What is it?"

Allie pulled a jump rope out of her back pocket.

"This!" she shouted.

"*This* looks like a jump rope to me, not a genius plan," said Amy.

"But wait till you see what we *do* with it," said Allie. She bent down and tied their ankles together. "Now I can't go to camp. I *have* to stay here with you."

"This is so wacky," said Amy.

"This is so *us*," said Allie. The girls began to walk with the jump rope tied around their ankles.

Step . . .

step . . .

step . . .

"It's working," said Amy. "This is fun!"

Step . . . step . . . step . . .

"See, I *am* a genius!" said Allie.

Step . . . step . . . step . . .

Boom! Down they went.

"Ouch!" said Amy.

The two friends got up. They tried again. This time they went more carefully.

Step . . . inside feet. Step . . . outside feet. Step . . . inside feet. Step . . . outside feet.

"We've got it!" said Allie.

"Together!" said Amy.

"Forever!" said Allie.

They walked faster and faster.
On their third trip around the
block, they were really zooming.
As they turned the corner, they
bumped right into . . .

"MARVIN!!!"

yelled Allie and Amy. "Why
don't you watch where you're
going?"

"Watch where *I'm* going? Watch
where *you're* going," said Marvin.

Marvin bent down to pick up his skateboard. When he saw their ankles tied together, he started laughing.

"Hey, what's goofy and has three legs?" he asked. He did not wait for an answer. "It's you! You look like a three-legged kooky bird."

"Oh, really? There's no such thing as a kooky bird," said Amy.

"Exactly," said Marvin. "So, how come you're tied together?"

"If you must know, Mr. Marvin Q. Smarty-Pants, being tied together is part of a genius plan to prevent our summer **separation**," said Allie.

"Separation? No *way*," said Marvin. "You two are glued together."

"Yes *way*," said Allie. "It's too horrible even to think about."

"It's definitely too horrible to talk about," said Amy. "We're leaving!"

Allie and Amy put their noses in the air and stomped away. Inside feet. Outside feet. Inside feet. Outside feet.

"Bye-bye, kooky bird!" called Marvin.

The girls played together the rest of the afternoon, then headed home. When they got to their street, Amy's mother called, "Amy! It's time for supper!"

Amy took a step toward her building. Something was pulling her back. It was Allie. For a minute, Amy had forgotten all about being tied to her.

"I guess we have to eat together. What are you having for supper?" asked Amy.

"My mother's making fish fry," said Allie.

"**Eewww!** Smelly. I hate that!" said Amy. "Why don't you come to my house?"

"What are you having?" asked Allie.

"I'm not too sure," said Amy. "But I know it's leftovers, and it's green."

"**Eewww!**" said Allie. "You know I don't eat green!"

"Well, I'm hungry," said Amy.

"Me too," said Allie.

"Maybe this isn't such a genius plan after all," said Amy.

"Maybe you're right," said Allie. She sighed, then bent down and untied the jump rope.

Allie and Amy said good-bye and went into their buildings.

That night, both of them had trouble sleeping. In two days Allie was going to camp—without Amy!

5

Tick! Tick! Tick!

"Today is our last day together," Amy said gloomily the next morning.

"That's why we have to get busy," said Allie.

"Doing what?" asked Amy.

"Everything! We have to do everything on our list!" Allie exclaimed, waving the list in the air.

"But we can't do it all in one day," said Amy.

"Yes, we can. We just have to move fast. We already visited Madame Lulu," said Allie, crossing it off the list.

"The next thing is the Spring Street Fair," said Amy.

"Are you ready?" said Allie.

"Ready!" said Amy.

"On your mark, get set, go!" cried Allie.

Amy and Allie raced around the corner to the fair. There was music playing, and the street was filled with games, rides, food to eat, and things to buy.

"This is great! Let's get our faces painted! Let's go on the Ferris wheel! Let's win a windup fish!" said Amy.

"Okay, but we'd better set the alarms on our watches," said Allie.

"I have to pack for camp this afternoon."

Amy and Allie set their watches. In half an hour their alarms would beep.

They went to the face-painting

table first. A friendly lady with a rose on her cheek asked what they wanted.

"I want a puppy!" said Amy.

"I'll get a kitten!" said Allie.

The lady painted their faces. Allie and Amy looked great together, *and* they had sixteen whole minutes left!

They raced to the Ferris wheel. Before long they were swinging in a basket way up high. They

could look out over the whole fair.

"Hey, I see the fishbowl game," said Amy.

When the Ferris wheel stopped, the friends had eight minutes left.

They ran straight to the game booth. But there was a long line.

Tick, tick, tick. Three minutes went by. *Tick, tick, tick.* Three more minutes went by.

By the time the man behind the counter called "Next!" they had only two minutes left.

Allie and Amy walked up to the booth together.

"Four throws for fifty cents," said the man.

Allie and Amy each gave the man a coin and each got two balls.

Amy went first. She knew she had to work fast. She tried not to look at her watch.

"Okay, ball, go into the bowl. Win me a windup fish!" she said.

Amy was trying to throw quickly. She threw the ball too hard. It went sailing across the street.

"Take it easy," said the man.

"I'll try," said Amy. **"But I'm in a hurry!"**

She threw the second ball. The man ducked just in time.

"Let me try! It's my turn," said Allie. Her first ball landed way over in the Space Rocket ride. They watched the ball disappear into the Moon Tunnel.

"Hurry!" said Amy. "Our time is almost up."

"I'm hurrying!" shouted Allie. She threw the last ball. It bounced off the wall of the booth and landed right on a cone of cotton candy— guess whose cotton candy?

"MARVIN!!!

Why don't you watch where you're walking?" shouted Allie and Amy together.

"Watch where I'm *walking*? Watch where you're *throwing*!"

yelled Marvin. He ran over to them.

Beep-beep. Beep-beep. Beep-beep.

"What's all that beeping?" asked Marvin. "You two really are goofy."

"No, we really are organized," said Allie. "Those beeps were our watch alarms. That means we have to go now. Bye!"

She grabbed Amy's arm and dragged her out of the fair.

6

Splash!

"Come on, Amy. We have to skate and sing backward. That's next on the list," said Allie as they headed home.

"What's after that?" asked Amy.

"Swimming at the town pool,"

said Allie. "We'd better hurry!"

Allie and Amy raced upstairs and came back down with skates on their feet and bathing suits under their clothes.

They headed for the pool, skating backward and singing to

the tune of "The Star-Spangled Banner," *"Be can we silly how, see you can say, oh!"*

After stumbling quite a few times on skates and words, Allie and Amy finally made it to the pool. They tossed their things into lockers and headed out for some fun.

Standing at the edge of the deep end, Allie called, "One, two, three, jump!"

Splash! As soon as they were in, they swam underwater

all the way to the shallow end. They swam right into a pair of feet. These looked like the very same feet they'd seen walking around at the fair.

Allie and Amy popped up out of the water.

"MARVIN!!!"

cried Allie. "Why don't you watch where you're standing?"

"Watch where I'm *standing*? Watch where you're *swimming*!" said Marvin.

"We have to be at this end of the pool. We're going to play Marco Polo," said Allie.

"Well, this end of the pool is taken," said Marvin.

Allie and Amy looked at each other and nodded.

"It just so happens, we need three players," said Amy. "Marvin, you can be *it*."

"Me? It? Sorry, I just forgot how to play," said Marvin.

"Let us remind you," said Allie. "You close your eyes and call out, 'Marco.' Then we say, 'Polo,' and you have to catch us."

"Let me think about it," said Marvin, getting a funny look on his face—funnier than usual.

Then he said, "Okay, I'll play."

He closed his eyes, but instead of calling out "Marco," he called, **"Martha!"**

"That's not funny," said Amy, trying not to laugh.

"So sorry," said Marvin. "I'll try again." He closed his eyes and called, **"Macaroni!"**

Allie got a gleam in her eye. She was supposed to answer, "Polo!" Instead she said, "Cheese!"

Now Amy got the idea. "Tomato sauce!" she called.

Marvin splashed through the water after Amy. Amy slipped past him.

"Massachusetts!" called Marvin.

Amy tried to think of a state.

"Michigan!" she called.

"Minnesota!" called Allie
from a corner of the pool.

Marvin dived in Allie's direc-
tion. His hand swatted her toe.

"You're *it!*" he shouted.

It was Allie's turn to close her eyes and call out, "Marco." Instead she closed her eyes and called, "Marvin!"

"The Great!" Marvin answered.

Amy groaned loudly.

"Gotcha!" said Allie, tagging Amy.

Beep-beep. Beep-beep. Beep-beep. The girls' alarms went off.

"Oh no, not again," said Marvin.

"We're very busy people," said Allie, rushing out of the pool. "I'm going to camp tomorrow. I've got to get home and pack," she called over her shoulder.

"What camp?" called Marvin.

But Allie and Amy were already too far away to hear him. They quickly dried off and jumped into their clothes. Then they headed home.

Allie and Amy stood in front of their buildings. They looked at their list. They had crossed off the first four things. There was still number five: *Make a new list of things to do.*

"I guess there's no point in making up a new list now," said Amy.

"I guess not," said Allie. "We can make another list when I come home."

Allie and Amy just stood there. Neither one wanted to go inside.

Then Amy's mother called to her, "Amy! **Please come upstairs!**"

"I guess I'd better go," said Amy. "I'll miss you, but I'll write. I promise."

"Me too, and we'll be together again after the summer," said Allie.

"See you later, alligator," said Amy.

"In a while, crocodile," said Allie.

Amy and Allie hugged each other. Then they disappeared into their buildings.

7

Let's Go!

Ring! Ring! Allie hadn't been home five minutes when the telephone rang. It was Amy.

"Guess what! Guess what!" Amy shouted happily.

"What? What?" asked Allie.

"There was another opening at Camp Merry Moose," said Amy. "And *I'm* going!"

"Hooray!" yelled Allie. "We are so lucky! I can't believe it."

"I've got to go pack," said Amy. "I'm so excited!"

"Me too," said Allie. "See you tomorrow!"

The next morning, the families met outside and walked around the corner to the bus stop. Allie and Amy skipped ahead, singing and holding hands.

The camp bus was waiting for them. The girls hugged their parents and jumped onto the bus.

They stopped at the door and waved, calling, "Bye, Mom! Bye, Dad!"

Just then, they heard the sound

of skateboard wheels scraping the sidewalk.

"Look, it's Marvin," said Amy.

"You know, I'm going to kind of miss him," said Allie. "He can be **obnoxious**, but he's pretty funny, too."

"You're right," said Amy. "It was fun playing Marco Polo with him. Oh well, we'll see him when we get back."

Allie and Amy found two seats together on the bus.

"Oh, Marvin! Here's your camp

bag," called Marvin's mother, running after him.

Amy looked at Allie. Allie looked at Amy.

"Did she say '*camp* bag'?" asked Amy.

"It isn't possible!" said Allie.

But it *was* possible. Marvin got on the bus wearing a Camp Merry Moose T-shirt!

Allie's foot was sticking out in the aisle. ***Boom!*** Marvin tripped right over it.

"MARVIN!!!

Why don't you watch where you put your feet?" said Allie.

"Watch where I put *my* feet? Watch where you put *yours*!" said Marvin.

"Eewww, look out, Allie," cried Amy, ducking down in her seat. "There's a big googly-eyed bug climbing up Marvin's T-shirt!"

Marvin jumped back and started brushing at his shirt.

"Gotcha!" said Amy.

Marvin's face turned bright red. "You got me this time. But we've got a *whole* summer," he said, smiling. "I'll get you back."

Suddenly a familiar sound filled the air. *Clink!* Then a familiar voice called, "Buckle up, everyone. We're off to Camp Merry Moose!"

"It isn't possible!" said Amy.

But it *was* possible. Madame Lulu had just stepped onto the bus!

"Hi, Madame Lulu! What are you doing here?" called Amy.

"I looked into my crystal ball. It said I would be going to a special place. And I am. I'm the Camp Merry Moose **drama** counselor," explained Madame Lulu.

"Wow!" Amy whispered to Allie. "She even tells her own fortune."

"Okay, kids!" called the

bus driver. "We're on our way!"

The driver closed the doors and started the motor. As soon as she did, some kids started to sing the Camp Merry Moose bus song. In no time, everyone was singing together.

"Let's go, let's go
to Camp Merry Moose!
It's time to have fun.
Just turn us loose.
Our camp is the best.
It beats all the rest."

Suddenly a paper airplane marked *M* flew toward Allie's and Amy's heads. They each ducked just in time. A few seconds later—**Clink! Clink!**—Madame Lulu was swatting the airplane off her head.

"This summer is going to be so much fun," said Amy.

"We're going to need a new list of things to do, after all," said Allie.

Allie took out paper and a pencil.

"Number one. Learn to sail," she said.

"Number two. Make things at arts and crafts," said Amy.

"Number three. Star in Madame Lulu's play," said Allie. She stopped with her pencil in the air. "What else do you do at camp?" she asked.

"I don't know," said Amy.

"How about this for number four?" said Allie. She wrote in great big letters:

HAVE THE BEST SUMMER EVER!

"That will be easy," said Amy.

"For us," said Allie.

"Because we're together," said Amy.

"Forever!" said Allie.

And they gave high fives as the bus bounced down the road.

Word List

burst (BERST): Sprang out or said suddenly

crumpled (CRUM·pulled): Crushed

drama (DRAH·muh): The activity of performing in a play, movie, or TV show

hazy (HAY·zee): Cloudy or misty

humid (HYOO·mid): Damp or steamy

husky (HUH·skee): Sounding deep and rough

obnoxious (ob·NOK·shus): Annoying or unpleasant

palms (POLMS): The flat inner parts of the hands between the wrists and the bases of the fingers

perked (PURKT): Became lively or cheerful

seekers (SEE·kers): People who are trying to find something

separation (seh·puh·RAY·shun): The act of moving apart

shivers (SHIH·vers): Body shakes

trance (TRANCE): A sleeplike state during which one is not fully aware

veil (VALE): A thin piece of cloth worn to cover one's face

yelped (YELPT): Said with a short, sharp cry

Questions

1. What makes a friendship special? Name three things that matter to you.
2. If you went to see Madame Lulu, what would you ask her?
3. When you have an important question, who's the person you go to?
4. It worked out great when Allie and Amy gave Marvin a chance to join them doing something fun. Is there

someone you'd like to get to know better? What would you invite that person to do?

5. What's your idea of the best summer ever?

LOOKING FOR A FAST, FUN READ? BE SURE TO MAKE IT ALADDIN QUIX!

CHUCKLE YOUR WAY THROUGH THESE EASY-TO-READ ILLUSTRATED CHAPTER BOOKS!

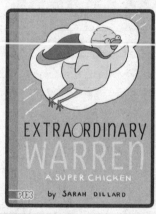

EBOOK EDITIONS ALSO AVAILABLE